TEMBO'S ROAR

IAIN GOW

TEMBO'S ROAR

a Spiritual Journey of Discovery

Illustrated by MARK ROUSE

Tembo's Roar
Published by Iain Gow
New Zealand

© 2019 Iain Gow

ISBN 978-0-473-47684-7 (Softcover)
ISBN 978-0-473-47685-4 (ePUB)
ISBN 978-0-473-47686-1 (Kindle)

Illustration:
Mark Rouse

Editing & Production:
Andrew Killick
Castle Publishing Services
www.castlepublishing.co.nz

Cover design:
Paul Smith

To Sam and Matt, my boys,
and the next generation of cousins:
may you seek, trust in the journey,
and may you come to bless the world with
the gifts you have been given.

And to Linda, my 'anam cara' (my soul friend),
who has loved me in 'sickness and in health',
in wobbly bits and in joy!

FOREWORD

The story of Tembo is a story of transformation; transformation of individual lives and of societies. With its biblical overtones and a strong African setting, the reader is drawn into an opportunity to examine some of the greatest issues we face in our conflicted world.

Tembo's Roar will capture the imagination of children, and of the adults who read the story to them or with them. Together they will easily move to explore some of the big questions of life and death, of life's values and purpose.

For the author, Iain Gow, there is an element of autobiography here. And many others of us will likewise see aspects of our own life's journey, our fears and our hopes, all under the fascinating guise of Lionkind.

So let your imagination roam free, and let your spirit soar and encounter the transforming power of love and the mysterious workings of the divine.

The Right Reverend Ross Bay
Bishop of Auckland

T*embo's Roar: A Spiritual Journey of Discovery* is about living life to the full, ready for the final journey to the final embrace – 'te taanga manawa', in te reo Maori – where everyone experiences beautiful light and beautiful roars, true voices and familiar faces.

Tembo's journey through life bursts with short episodes of suffering and happiness, loneliness and fulfilment, being crushed to rising again, defeat and victory, despair and hope, and sadness and joy.

What Tembo cherished, like other young lions, was the story of the Great Lion, Ballo. Ballo stands for all that is good and noble; honour and power; mana, ihi, wehi and wana. Ballo brings peace and puts an end to evil. He gives strength to the lion world, especially to young lions, who gain inspiration and hope from him.

Alone one day and deeply saddened by life events, Tembo prays to Ballo out of desperation and his world changes. He experiences incredible love, and feels a force of peace and kindness which heals him, his body and eventually his heart.

Ballo gives Tembo his mission to create a kingdom of peace. The young lion rises up to the challenge to confront evil. Through his bravery and Ballo's love, the power of love defeats the love of power, making possible forgiveness and reconciliation.

I came to know Iain Gow when he was the director of Vaughan Park Anglican Retreat Centre. His experience of having lived in different parts of the world prepared him well to work with many cultures and languages, including

Maori. He brought an understanding to his ministry that allowed us to be fully aware that we were in a sacred place – a place of prayer, reflection, rest and hospitality. That same heart is evident in this book. I personally valued his friendship and collegiality, and appreciated very much his gifts of leadership and priestly discernment.

I commend this book to you.

The Right Reverend Te Kitohi Wiremu Pikaahu
Bishop Tai Tokerau

CONTENTS

PREFACE

I first started writing the story of Tembo in 1986, while living in Belgium as a young professional working for a pharmaceutical company, and I had many questions about life and faith.

My father came to visit from Guernsey and asked whether we could go to a local church on Sunday morning. I didn't think that was a good idea, but I went along for his sake. The person who met us at the door of the church was the managing director of Amex, Benelux. He played guitar in the worship band. He was called John and he and his wife, Anne, welcomed me into their home over the months that followed. They nurtured me. Around the same time, I met a young woman named Sarah, who saw the potential Iain, and introduced me to her God.

Positively influenced by these three friends, I slowly and very tentatively began to explore the Christian faith. I was seeking to find out if there was something or someone bigger than myself, beyond my understanding – transcendent and yet full of longing for intimacy with all creation. I'm now a follower of Christ, but over thirty years later, like Tembo, I'm still an explorer!

When I had finished that first version of the Tembo story, I sent it off to some publishers in America, but never received a reply. A year or so later, the film *Lion King* came out, and I knew I was beat!

Enough water has passed under the bridge since then, so I thought now would be a good time for Tembo to be released into the wild. After thirty years, I reconnected with the illustrator, Mark, a very dear friend of mine from my days at the University of Denver in USA. (We received our black belts in Taekwondo together, but that is now a distant youthful memory!) I handed the manuscript over to Castle Publishing. (I would very much like to thank them, and especially Andrew Killick, for the way he has counselled me through this process of writing, bettering the story by his advice.) The result of all this is the book you now hold in your hands.

Whether you have a Christian faith, are unsure, or have another faith, I hope you (and your children) will enjoy the story of Tembo.

———————

Iain is also the author of *Be Still,* a book of prayers illustrated by Nat Tate. About 3000 copies of this have been distributed. If you would like to buy one, please email gow.iain@yahoo.com or visit www.castlepublishing.co.nz

CHARACTERS & PLACES IN THE STORY

Below is guide to how to say the words that appear in this book. Feel free to use these pronunciations or have fun making up your own.

Tembo (pronounced *Tem-bow*)
Marumba (pronounced *Ma-rruuum-ba*)
Jagola Mountains (pronounced *Ja-goor-la*)
Ballo (pronounced *Baa-lo*)
Nembonja (pronounced *Nem-bon-cha*)
Otamangi Swamp (pronounced *Ota-maa-ngi*)
Chichi (pronounced *Chee-chee*)
Omkhulu (pronounced *Om-cool-shla*)
Ncane (impossible to pronounce so just try your best!)

Chapter 1

TEMBO'S BIRTH

Tembo's birth came to pass in a confused way. It was winter's turn to bring snow, but spring had decided all by itself to come early.

Beautiful flowers sprouted, rivers fizzed with clean water, squirrels forgot they were meant to be hoarding their nuts, and into this world of colour, Tembo was born to Marumba.

Marumba only carried one lion in the pregnancy. That was unusual for a lion.

Marumba had missed Tembo's father, Ganjo, while she was pregnant with Tembo. She remembered how Ganjo had fought seven other lions for her paw in marriage. He had cared deeply for her. But six months ago, he was taken from her.

Together they had been prowling for food, when suddenly five lions of the Mumba tribe had pounced from the long grass of the plains and killed him.

She would have been killed too, with the baby inside her, but Ganjo had given his life for her. He had shouted to her to escape and, in that moment, she knew she would not see him again, until she joined him in the Jagola Mountains, lion heaven, one day.

The last few months had been sad without her beloved Ganjo. But one day, there was a movement in her tummy. She knew the time had come. She went to the cave Ganjo had chosen, and there she gave birth to her cub.

Chapter 2

TEMBO'S FIRST GROWL

Tembo's first growl was not a growl befitting someone special. It was more of a squeak.

The rest of the lion pack had gathered around the mouth of the cave when they heard the news of Tembo's birth. For some reason, the new-born cub made them feel happy. He had a twinkle in his eye! They kissed Marumba good night and left two strong young lions to guard her cave during the night in case any pesky hyenas came sniffing for food.

At first, Tembo felt very shaky on his legs. He wanted to go one way, but when he put his chubby legs and paws forward, off they went in another direction. You may have had the same problems when you first tried to walk!

In time though, he became stronger and his growl became a bit fiercer. It was good to be alive! This new and exciting world was full of weird and wonderful things. Take, for example, the skunk's smell when it farted because it had eaten too much!

But alongside these thrilling new sights, smells and sensations, Tembo felt something was missing.

Chapter 3

TEMBO'S HEARTACHE

In the middle of him, deep inside, where all Tembo's emotions came and went, he felt like there was a gap, and he couldn't work out what it was.

One day when he was playing with his friend, Junga, he realised he was different. Junga had a dad, and they had 'dad talks' at night.

Tembo missed 'dad talks'. Sadly he dragged his paws back to the place where he and his mother slept. It wasn't like Tembo to look so down. Marumba nuzzled in close and asked him what was wrong.

She listened deeply to Tembo's heart-cry for a dad, then carefully she said to the young lion cub, 'Tembo, you can still have "dad talk" because your dad is always near you through his love.'

'How do I know that he loves me when I can't see him?' asked Tembo, with the smallest of voices.

'Well,' Murumba said, 'one day you will go to the Jagola Mountains – the special place just beyond where you can see. There, you will speak to him face to face, but for now, any time you want a "dad talk," just lift your eyes up to the sky, and know that your father loves you more than the furthest cloud away, further than the furthest place in space, beyond all the stars.'

That is a lot of love! thought Tembo. *I am mightily loved!* And from that day, he always knew his dad was close by, helping him with love greater than the distance of the furthest star.

Chapter 4

OFF TO SCHOOL

Lions go to lion school when they reach a certain age. Tembo learnt about different plants and animals, how it was important to grow up and help others, and how never to waste food.

The most interesting lesson was on snakes, which slithered on the ground.

The black mamba was the meanest, as it gave a nasty bite.

The cobra always went for your eyes! 'Paws up,' was the instruction the young lions were given. When you saw a cobra, you quickly had to hide your eyes behind your paws, so the snake could not spit at you and make you blind. If you weren't fast enough to cover your face, then the only thing that helped was washing out your eyes with milk. For that, you had to find a cow, and lions and cows didn't go together most times!

The exams were hard, but after a long day at school, the lion cubs would come back with their teachers, sit around the camp-fire, and listen to the lion elders tell exciting stories. In this way they received wisdom from those who had come before.

Chapter 5

BALLO THE GREAT LION

One story the lion cubs loved hearing around the fire was the story of Ballo and Nembonja, for it was a story about good and evil.

It was said that Ballo had come from the Jagola Mountains. All the animals of the Animal Kingdom knew that the Jagola Mountains were a special place. It was where a lion's spirit travelled when they ended their life on earth.

Ballo was the Great Lion. He had always lived, he had always been, since before all time had started. And he would be there after it finished.

Ballo had a mission; it was to be costly, but all missions of the heart make you vulnerable.

The mission was to bring peace to the world of the lions, because they had forgotten how to live and love.

Ballo came to show a different way, but first he had to defeat Nembonja!

Chapter 6

NEMBONJA THE EVIL CROCODILE

The Otamangi Swamp, explained the lion elders, as the young lions listened in the flickering light of the fire, was a misty, murky place – a forgotten place of shadows. It was the lair of Nembonja the crocodile, who was feared by all animals.

Most crocodiles are brownish in colour, but Nembonja was more sinister-looking than the blackest black widow spider. He was so fierce that even the Kaljo (a yellowish crocodile), Manjo (a greenish crocodile) and Voljo (a red crocodile) were terrified of him and kept out of his way.

Nembonja was very evil. His innocent prey would see a shadow in the water, then – teeth! His fangs were the length of three hands. His tail was as long as a tall palm tree. His body was covered in an amour of huge scales.

Nembonja did not have a friend in the world. Except one – a small bird called Chichi – but even she didn't really count as a friend, because Nembonja kept trying to eat her.

Nonetheless, Chichi stayed close by.

Theirs was a strange friendship and, even today, every so often if you look out your window, just before you go to bed, you might see Chichi riding on the back of Nembonja's mighty tail.

Chapter 7

CHICHI, FRIEND OF NEMBONJA

The young lions shifted uneasily as they listened to the lion elders. Nembonja didn't sound like a crocodile you would want to meet.

'Tell us about Chichi,' asked one of the young lions, hoping to change the subject.

'Well,' the lion elder said, falling for the question, 'Chichi, the little bird, was known for her large beak. Sometimes her beak got in the way, but at other times it was very helpful for catching tasty little grubs.'

She belonged to the Tiki Tiki family – a very brave and snooty family. Tiki Tiki birds are not frightened of any of the animals in the animal kingdom – not the hippo-poto-mighta-moses, nor even the rhino-charger.

Each Tiki Tiki bird has a dangerous job: they must place themselves in the big animal's mouth. Then, like a little dentist, they must clean and fix all the big animal's teeth. But if they make one wrong move – snap! The Tiki Tiki could be finished.

Without Tiki Tiki birds, big animals like the hippo-poto-mighta-moses and the rhino-charger would get sore teeth. And if that happens, they get very grumpy. Even worse, they charge around all over the place, causing a lot of dust. No one likes that!

Chichi's talent was that she was even smaller than other Tiki Tiki birds, and she was clever. She would dart into Nembonja's mouth to clean his teeth. But whenever he tried to gobble her up, Chichi, who was not afraid of the dark, would just let him chomp down.

Chichi would hide in his mouth, away from Nembonja's sharp fangs, and give him a tickle on his tongue with her beak. Nembonja, trying hard not to laugh, would open his jaws, and out would pop Chichi, unharmed!

Chapter 8

THE MIGHTY BATTLE

Chichi may have been able to make Nembonja laugh, but the day Ballo and Nembonja met, there was no laughter. The animal kingdom went silent and everyone held their breath for a very long time.

When Ballo, the Great Lion, arrived from the Jagola Mountains, he travelled to Nembonja's lair. Within the dark swirly waters of the Otamangi Swamp swam many beasts that were distant cousins to Nembonja and had no names.

To have no name is a very sad thing indeed, because our names tell us who we are. Also, have you ever tried to get someone's attention with no name? It's hard!

Ballo had come to battle evil so that even evil could be transformed into good.

When Nembonja and Ballo fought their great battle, the ground shook for forty days and nights. It was a battle between life and death.

In the end, Ballo stood victorious (how that happened is another story) and Nembonja promised to change his ways.

He joined Ballo in bringing peace to the animal kingdom. From that day onwards, Ballo was able to ride across the kingdom on Nembonja's long tail and spread his message of love.

Nembonja's swamp became a place of hope, no longer a place of despair.

Chapter 9

TEMBO & THE WILD BOAR

Tembo grew. His days were filled with lessons at school, and more stories around the fire at night.

Then suddenly, with the passage of time, it was his fifteenth birthday – the day a lion leaves his cub years behind and becomes an adult! Now he was allowed to hunt by himself.

Tembo travelled far that day, and eventually came to a cliff overhanging a river. He knew he was outside the territory of his lion tribe, so he kept his senses sharp.

He spotted a buck, leapt forward and began his chase.

But something wasn't right. Tembo came to a stop in a cloud of dust and lifted his nose to the wind. He turned to his left and saw a huge wild boar, with two long tusks that had seen many battles, given the scars and chips in them, snorting and staring at him. Tembo was being tracked!

When the boar realised Tembo had spotted him, he gave up trying to be sneaky and charged directly at the young lion.

Thoughts rushed through Tembo's head, but before he could move, the boar slammed hard into his shoulder.

The attacker's tusks had drawn blood, and Tembo knew he had to do something quickly – there would be no second chance.

The wild boar stepped back, then charged again. At the last moment, Tembo flattened himself to the ground and the boar sailed over him, catapulting over the cliff and far down into the river below.

Tembo felt relieved but weak from the wound in his shoulder. He thought about the lessons his mother and the elders had taught him. He found the Manjoorabooya plant, with its special healing powers, and lay on it. Eventually the pain started to ease, but he was so, so tired.

Tembo's head drooped onto his front paws, and while he slept, he felt a strange warmth surrounding him that seemed to come from far away – beyond where he could see – from the Jagola Mountains.

Tembo awoke with a start. It was late in the afternoon, and he knew the other lions in his tribe, and his mother, would be worried about where he was. The blood had stopped, and even though his shoulder felt stiff, he knew he could walk slowly.

He thanked the Manjooraboya plant for its kindness, then started for home. He wanted to tell Junga and his other friends how he had defeated the wild boar. He was so hungry; he thought he could eat at least three zebras!

Chapter 10

THE BREAKING OF TEMBO'S HEART

As Tembo neared home, his excitement rose about telling the story of his adventure, and his stomach growled as he thought about the big meal he'd soon be eating. But as he rounded a huge rock, his heart dropped inside him and his legs weakened. Poor Tembo – he had such a big spirit but so much still to learn.

Before him, on the ground, lay many dead lions. A huge battle had taken place while he was away. He looked around and saw many faces he recognised – it seemed his entire tribe had been lost. Lions from the Mumba tribe were also lying among those who had died.

He knew immediately what this must mean.

Tembo had been taught that, once upon a time, all lion tribes had lived together peacefully, until one day, two brothers had fought. Their names were Omkhulu (meaning the big one, and pronounced Om-cool-shla) and Ncane (meaning the small one, and impossible to pronounce so just try your best). The elders had sent them both away to re-discover love instead of jealousy, but instead of turning his heart towards good, Omkhulu, the older brother, became angry and left for the north.

For a long time, nothing was heard of him, but then messages started coming back that Omkhulu had made himself king of the north. He was known to have a cruel heart and his aim was to smash all the other lion tribes until he reigned supreme.

Tembo realised that he wasn't safe. Perhaps some of Omkhulu's warriors were still prowling nearby. But he was so sad, he couldn't move. He didn't care. He saw Junga's body. Then he saw his mother, and his heart broke even more. He went and lay beside her. He sniffed her, but he knew that she was gone. Tears came to his eyes. He stroked her gently with his paws, then nuzzled his face into her soft coat. 'Please don't leave me; I love you so much,' he whispered.

Chapter 11

TEMBO PRAYS FOR HELP

Tembo gave up. He lay at this mother's side for a long time. He didn't care about anything.

Then an unexpected thought came into Tembo's mind. He knew that the old tales about Ballo, the Great Lion from the Jagola Mountains, were probably just a myth. But he was alone, he had no other help, and what harm could it do?

I will call out to Ballo, he thought to himself, *and see if anything happens.*

'Ballo,' he prayed in a tired whisper, 'if you are real, please help me.' And with that, he closed his eyes, his hope all but gone.

Nothing seemed to happen – the wind still blew across the silent plains – but unknown to Tembo, Ballo had heard the young lion's prayers and responded to Tembo's broken heart.

Sometimes prayers seem not to be heard. This is a mystery that is difficult to understand, but we should keep on praying, because sometimes the answer has a long way to travel. And sometimes the answer suddenly appears.

Chapter 12

NEMBONJA SAVES TEMBO

Suddenly, the earth shook like jelly in a bowl. Thunder erupted over Tembo's head. He stood up with a fright. Then there was complete quiet. A small bird stood before him – a Tiki Tiki – and behind the bird stood a huge black crocodile.

'Hello,' said the bird, 'I am Chichi! That ugly crocodile can never make a quiet entrance.' Chichi rolled his eyes and shook his head.

Tembo wondered if he was dreaming.

The crocodile opened his huge jaws and a rumble came out. 'I have come for you,' he said. 'In former days, you would have made a tasty snack, but you are so scrawny, I'm not interested.'

Tembo wasn't sure if he should run.

'Only joking,' the crocodile said, and his massive fangs glinted in the sun. He seemed to be smiling. 'Ballo, who healed my evil and brings peace to all animals, has sent me to you.'

Tembo didn't know what to say! He had heard the myth of the crocodile that was tamed by a lion, but it was just a story, wasn't it? Could this be Nembonja standing in front of him?

Tembo simply stared, until Chichi gave him a tickle with her beak and said, 'Hop onto his tail, come on. Hold tight.'

Tembo turned and looked sadly at his mother – he didn't want to leave her – but something deep inside him knew his destiny was calling him to respond to Chichi's invitation.

Nembonja and Chichi seemed to understand Tembo's sadness, but Nembonja rumbled in a way that almost sounded kind, 'Tembo, this is the way.' Tembo nuzzled his mother's body one last time, then he and Chichi climbed aboard Nembonja's huge scaly tail.

Chapter 13

TEMBO MEETS BALLO

Nembonja moved quickly, but the journey was long. At the end of two days' travelling, they came to a bright light in the darkness. It was welcoming, warm and friendly.

From the distance, an old but very majestic lion came out to meet him.

Tembo crouched in a low bow because he immediately knew, with every fibre of his being, who the lion was. It was Ballo himself – the King of the animals, the Great Lion from the Jagola Mountains.

'Welcome, my young friend,' said Ballo in a voice that made Tembo tremble and feel warm all at the same time. 'I know you feel very lost. That's because love makes you fragile. In time though, that same fragile love will heal you.'

Tembo looked up into Ballo's face and was mesmerised. It was Ballo's eyes... the most incredible love came from them – a force that was filled with peace and kindness and called things back to life.

Tembo hoped Ballo had a miracle for him. He was so weary from the pain he carried in his heart.

Ballo blew a gentle soft breath towards Tembo. Suddenly Tembo lifted off the ground – he and Ballo were flying! Was he really flying or did he just feel like he was flying because Ballo's love surrounded him, was deep inside him?

He let himself go, and time and space moved inside themselves and became many beautiful colours that healed.

He felt the wind in his mane. They seemed to be over water, and at last Ballo pointed into the distance and smiled at Tembo, as a beautiful green island appeared over the horizon.

Chapter 14

TEMBO & JEMBO BECOME FRIENDS

Tembo paced to and fro, enjoying the feeling of the soft grass under his paws – it was like nothing he had ever felt before. He looked up as a female lion came bounding up to him with a smile.

Tembo felt a bit shy, but he tried a roar of greeting as she approached. Fortunately for lions, there are not lots of different languages like in the human world, where we have Maori, English, French and Russian.

'Hello,' said the young lioness, 'welcome to Ballo's island. My name is Jembo and my parents were also killed by the Mumba tribe. I too was left for dead, but Ballo found me and brought me here to this place of healing. I come from a range of mountains that lies to the east of the lake that never seems to end.'

Jembo was talkative and spoke very quickly in her strange accent, but Tembo liked the sound of her voice. Sometimes he had to interrupt and say, 'Please can you repeat what you said again, as I didn't understand.' Then he would laugh in an embarrassed way. She would just smile and nudge him with her shoulder.

As the days went by, Tembo began to feel his strength returning. It took some time, because not only his body, but also his heart, needed healing. In fact, his heart took longer to heal, but with Ballo's wise counsel, Tembo slowly began to find his way through the frightening and sad things that cluttered up his memories.

Apart from spending time in the presence of Ballo, Tembo enjoyed being with Jembo best of all. As he grew stronger, she took him exploring up and down the coast where they had great fun chasing ostriches. 'Such a silly bird,' they would say, 'it has huge wings but it can't fly!'

Chapter 15

TEMBO GETS A FUNNY FEELING IN HIS TUMMY

After a long day's exploring, Jembo would help Tembo pick out the brambles that got caught in his mane. She would often tell him what to do and she was a little bit bossy, but he didn't mind because she was so kind and friendly. Day by day, he found he liked her just a little bit more. He started to feel that gooey feeling where time seems to stretch when you are with someone you like a lot, but is still too short when you have to say goodbye.

Tembo felt completely upside down with all these new feelings. His paws would get tangled when he tried to do a pounce, and sometimes his mouth felt a bit dry when he tried to talk – especially when she looked directly at him. It was all very confusing.

Eventually he had to ask Ballo about it. Ballo chuckled with a twinkle in his eyes. 'Ah my young lion,' he said, 'so you are being introduced to the ways of love? Go slow my young lion, and you will know when you will know.'

Tembo didn't know what to make of that answer. *Why does Ballo always speak in such riddles?* he wondered.

Chapter 16

DUCKS...

Tembo strolled around under the big bushy trees. Silkworms had eaten little holes in some of the leaves so that the moonlight could shine through the thick foliage and give light to everyone who wanted to read before going to bed. The silkworms on Ballo's island were very clever; they knew just how much of the leaf to eat and how much to leave, so that the trees continued to grow and the ducks were able to have light.

Tembo went up to a tree and scratched his back against it. He felt an overwhelming surge of love flow through his body for all the trees and animals around him. For a long moment, he knew the beauty of heaven on earth, and all was well inside him.

Tembo let out a soft roar of contentment – nothing too hard or loud, mind you, because he didn't want to startle anyone or hurt their feelings.

The warm, fluffy-winged ducks sitting around on the grass under the trees eyed him carefully, not quite knowing what to think of the lion. But this was Ballo's island, and they felt safe, so with a quack here and a quack there, they closed their eyelids, tucked their beaks under their wings and fell asleep.

Well, not all of them. One old duck – 'Quacka' by name – who had just come to Ballo's island to heal, kept one eye opened. He still wasn't too sure about this place, despite everything he had heard about animals living together in peace. But soon the soothing air of the island did its work, and slowly, despite every attempt to stay awake, his eye blinked shut. He let out a quack of happiness, and off he went to sleep.

Chapter 17

...AND DEW DROPS

T embo noticed Quacka and chuckled to himself. It would take some time before everyone learnt to trust each other completely.

The leaves rustled above him, and a few diamond drops of dew plonked down on his head, but Tembo didn't mind at all. Even though the droplets were a little bit cold and slipped down his mane, he knew they were just being friendly.

A lot had happened since Tembo had talked to Ballo about his feelings of love for Jembo. Tembo and Jembo had been married in a ceremony attended by all the animals. And then another miracle thing had happened – Jembo gave birth to three cubs. Now Tembo had a family of his own!

He often gave a low growl of happiness to say how proud he was. But sometimes Jembo got a little bit cross with him because his low growls woke the cubs when they were asleep.

Women lions! thought Tembo… if he wanted to growl because he was proud, he would growl! But perhaps a little bit further away next time because he didn't want Jembo to be cross. She might make him sleep outside the cave – and that, as any male lion knows, is not much fun!

Chapter 18

BALLO GIVES TEMBO HIS QUEST

In the distance, walking among the trees in the cool night air, Tembo saw Ballo coming towards him.

Tembo bowed as Ballo came near. 'Walk with me, Tembo,' said the Great Lion.

They walked together in silence for a while, then Ballo said, 'I know you have wondered why you were brought to this island. Well, now it is time for me to tell you.'

Ballo paused and sniffed the breeze before he carried on. 'During these last five years, Omkhulu, the leader of the Mumba tribe, has grown strong and has taken over most of the lion empire. Thousands have been killed. Omkhulu has gone mad with power.

'Tembo,' Ballo went on, 'your calling is to save the lion tribes, nothing less.'

Tembo stood still, staring at Ballo in disbelief, before he managed to say, 'But... how will *I* fight Omkhulu's evil? I am young and alone!'

'You will never know what strength is in you and available to you, Tembo, until you trust. Your name means: 'I trust in' – that is your calling. So claim it! Trust and believe with all hope that heaven can use your gifts.

'It is your decision, my young friend; my love cannot force you, for then I would be at odds with myself. But, if you accept the mission, Nembonja will take you to the Nkigola River – the big wide river that smiles despite its sadness – where you will find a small group of lions like yourself. They are brave, and they wait for you to lead them.'

Tembo awoke the next morning, his fur wet with dew. The ducks were still asleep, and he wondered if he had dreamt the things that Ballo had told him. He pondered the Great Lion's words.

Almost before he noticed she was there, Jembo came up to him, with the cubs trailing alongside her. Tembo started to speak, but Jembo said, 'Hush, Tembo. I too was visited by Ballo last night. I know what he has asked of you. I do not wish to be separated from you, but you must go. I will keep the cubs safe until we can be together again. Our love will keep us strong.'

Tembo wanted to say he could not and would not do it, but somewhere inside he knew that Jembo was right. Come what may, he would accept the Great Lion's quest.

Chapter 19

TEMBO & HIS BAND OF LIONS

O n the shore of the Nkigola River stood a small band of lions. Tembo climbed off Nembonja's long and scaly tail, thanked the crocodile for carrying him, and bid him farewell. Then he faced the group he had been called to lead. They looked each other up and down.

Eventually one lion stepped forward and extended his paw to Tembo. With a quiet but strong voice he said, 'Welcome, sir. I am Javolo, at your service.' And from that moment on, the little group of warriors grew more and more loyal to each other as the days went by.

The band of lions spent a few months moving deeper and deeper into Omkhulu's territory. Tembo began to grow into the leader Ballo had called him to be. Sometimes he felt unsure of himself and yet, alongside that, he felt a deep calm that came when he prayed. He knew Ballo heard him.

The little band became a strong pride and more lions joined them as their fame spread, and others heard about the message of hope and peace that Tembo carried. But there were many fights and skirmishes along the way as they encountered brigades of Omkhulu's warriors.

Tembo didn't like the way each battle meant more injury and death. He hated the idea of lion cousins and brothers fighting each other. Before any battle, he would always try to talk to his enemies. You see, Ballo had taught him that you must only use force as a last resort.

The seasons went by, and soon two years had passed. Tembo sat by himself under a tree near a river and thought about all the battles his lions had fought. He wondered why Omkhulu was so full of hatred, anger and jealousy.

Tembo changed his position and saw one of his scouts waving to him from the other side of the river. He quickly got up to see what the noise was about. Some of his captains rushed to him, and Javolo, who had become his most trusted general, announced in his quiet but strong voice that Omkhulu was marching towards them, leading an army one hundred times bigger than Tembo's band of brave young lions.

With this news, Tembo quickly called his generals and captains together. It was a meeting full of urgency, for they had to make up their minds what to do. Tembo's group was far too small to take on such an army in pitched battle. The generals suggested to Tembo that they should fall back into the mountains where they could gather their strength for another day. Having given their best advice, everyone sat in silence, expecting Tembo to agree to this strategy – but they were very wrong.

'My friends,' said Tembo at last, 'it is time for me to meet Omkhulu.'

Chapter 20

TEMBO'S COURAGE

'No! Sir, this cannot be!' they all shouted. 'We are outnumbered – how can we fight such a big army?'

'Javolo,' said Tembo, turning quietly to his trusted friend, 'I want to meet with Omkhulu – he and I – face to face. I am tired of the bloodshed. I want to look into his eyes and call him to a better way. If he does not want peace, then I will have to fight him. But if it comes to that, Ballo will be with me in spirit.'

The lions had seen the power of love work through Tembo before. They had seen how lions who once hated each other had become friends. But they still thought Tembo's plan was foolish, for Omkhulu was very devious.

Tembo's generals gathered around him; they knew they couldn't change his mind. 'Sir,' said Javolo, 'I will come with you, even if it means my death. You must have some-one at your side.'

'I have Ballo's power,' answered Tembo, 'but all the same, I welcome you, my friend of many battles.'

Chapter 21

THE BIG INDABA

It dawned a beautiful day. The birds were only just beginning to warm up their voices for their morning songs, and the sun was only just waking up from its night's sleep.

Tembo had stayed awake, but he felt fresh and ready to meet Omkhulu. It was the day of the Indaba – the meeting between them.

Ballo's power felt very close to Tembo. He knew that no matter what happened, he must stay close to that power. His strong limbs twitched with nervousness, but his mission was to bring peace to the lion world, and he would do that at any cost.

He thought about Jembo and the cubs whom he had not seen for so long; he missed them and loved them very much. Then he thought of his mother and father and hoped that they could somehow see him from where they were in the Jagola Mountains.

Both armies – Tembo's on one side and Omkhulu's on

the other – were decked out for battle, their banners fluttering gently in the breeze. In the large area of open ground between them stood the place of meeting – a little tent. By the door of the tent, stood Omkhulu, fearsome and large, flanked by one of his most trusted generals.

As Tembo walked towards the tent with Javolo, his little army let out a mighty roar. Tembo turned and said to them, 'My friends, I hope today all fighting will stop so that all lions may live well together. If Omkhulu does not listen, then I will have to fight him. If I die, you will have to escape before his mighty army reaches you. I ask you now to pray for my mission.'

The lions prayed.

Chapter 22

MOMENT OF TRUTH

Omkhulu had waited a long time to meet Tembo – this young upstart had been a thorn in his side for too long. He would give Tembo a chance to talk, then he would sink his claws into the troublemaker. It was time to finish Tembo and his army once and for all.

The flies buzzed around Omkhulu's ears, giving him a headache, so he swatted one of them with a giant paw and crushed it. *That is exactly what I will do with Tembo*, he thought, *crush him with my paw*. Omkhulu ran his tongue over his fangs and they were as sharp as ever. He felt his muscles and they bulged. No one had ever beaten him in paw to paw and tooth to tooth combat. The foolish young lion didn't know the trap he was walking into.

As Tembo approached the tent, Omkhulu came towards him. He had death written all over his face. His mane rose up on the back of his neck, and he growled loudly. *Why wait?* he thought. *I can just finish him off right now.* Then, without warning, he rushed at Tembo with his paws ready to strike.

In the moment before Omkhulu pounced, Tembo shouted out, 'Stop! I have come to talk. I do not want to fight. If our talking fails, then we can fight and to the death. But I have come because I want the killing of lions to cease. I trust in a different way to your way.'

Omkhulu halted in his tracks. He was amazed at the innocence of this young lion. He seemed so naïve. Omkhulu couldn't believe his ears. He decided to play along for a while and see what the young lion wanted to say. Then he would finish him off.

'You young up-start, you have walked into this valley, and you are surrounded by my army,' answered Omkhulu. 'There will only be one ruler, and that will be me! But say your little speech so I can tell others that I was gracious to the young lion before I killed him.' He raised his paw again to strike, pausing to allow Tembo his final words.

'I will say it again, Omkhulu. I do not want to fight,' said Tembo. 'I want the lion world to live in peace. Your ways are wrong. You will never be happy until you allow love to flow into your life.'

Omkhulu snorted – he had never heard such rubbish in all his life. He let out another mighty growl, then sprang towards his prey.

Light on his feet, Tembo swerved, but Omkhulu's paw caught his flank and left a gash in his side. In Omkhulu came again. But this time, Tembo dipped in a feint, and as Omkhulu went by him, he caught Omkhulu off-balance. Jumping on Omkhulu's back, Tembo pinned him down. Both lions panted heavily, and blood trickled from Tembo's wound.

Chapter 23

OVERCOME

Then a strange thing happened. It is hard to explain. As Omkhulu let out a roar of defiance under the weight of Tembo's hold, his heart suddenly grew quiet. Tembo's words had found a distant memory in him. He realised he had wasted his life in violence and anger, and now he was old.

Dark thoughts flooded back into his mind for a moment, and he tried to gather his strength once more to throw Tembo off. But then the tiredness returned. Tears formed in his eyes, and his evil seeped out of him.

Sensing Omkhulu's weakness, Tembo stepped back warily, fearing it might be another trick. But what had happened was real. Omkhulu was changed. Something good had happened when nobody expected it, just when the lions in Tembo's band thought that all was lost. The word humans use for that kind of thing is 'miracle'.

Omkhulu had lost his roar. And when a lion loses his roar, his death comes soon afterwards. Tembo wept for

Omkhulu, and all that he could have been, if only he had let go of his anger years before.

Omkhulu looked at Tembo and said, 'Tembo, bring peace to our land… and may Ballo forgive me.' Then, with a sigh that almost sounded like contentment, Omkhulu passed away.

Chapter 24

A NEW KINGDOM

Omkhulu's army was restless. They had seen their leader's fate. They stood uncertainly, ready to avenge Omkhulu's death and use their vast numbers to overpower Tembo's warriors if they were given the order.

But Tembo walked between the two armies and, drawing himself up to his full height, he said in a loud voice, 'Brothers, Ballo the Great Lion has seen fit to let the power of love overcome war this day. There has been too much pain among the lion tribes. Put down your paws. Let us live together as friends. Let us be one kingdom. From this day forward, let this valley be known as Mumbumgongolo – The Valley of Peace.'

The two armies stared at Tembo. Apart from the sound of the fluttering of their banners, there was silence in the air. And then suddenly, lions began putting down their paws as Tembo had asked them to do. Their expressions changed from the snarls of battle to smiles of welcome. Hearts that had only known the desire to kill, no longer felt like causing pain.

As the lions on either side walked towards each other, they were no longer two armies but one large happy crowd – the meeting of long-lost friends, cousins and brothers.

And thus, by Tembo's bravery and the power of Ballo's love, the Lion Kingdom entered a new age – an age when lions were united, and all could live without fear.

Chapter 25

THE BIG WELCOME

Tembo the Brave lived for a very long time and was loved by all the lions. He and Jembo added many more cubs to their family. Together they had a wonderful life.

The whole lion kingdom was at peace and food was plentiful. The seasons were not too hot or too cold. Each lion found peace under the shade of his tree. Tembo ruled simply and with wisdom. The lions thanked Ballo the Great Lion, who had been before all lions, from whom they had been created. Some even claimed to have seen him, walking with Tembo in the cool of the evening.

As Tembo grew older, his bones would ache, and even though the weather was warm, sometimes he would get a bit chilly. He realised Ballo was calling to him and his time was approaching. Soon he would make his journey to the Jagola Mountains.

One night, near the end of summer, Tembo was dozing off by the side of the river.

He felt a tap on his shoulder and then, before he knew it, he was being carried into another time, far over rivers and plains to another world.

At first there was darkness – a big, black, fuzzy darkness, and he couldn't see properly. His fur went damp and his ears dropped down.

Then he felt a growing warmth surround him. He felt safe – completely and utterly safe. His eyes opened, as if for the first time, and all around him were gigantic mountains and valleys covered in beautiful flowers. Everything was bathed in the most beautiful light. He let out a roar of pleasure. He realised his roar sounded more like his true voice than it had ever sounded while he lived on earth. Then he heard a voice saying,

'Do not be afraid for you will never be alone.'

He practised his roar again, then realised that the sun seemed to be smiling down on him. *It feels like a friend,* he thought. He wanted to say hello and give it a hug. With that, he stretched, relaxed and let out the most beautiful roar he had ever made.

Tembo was shocked and happy at the outcome. His roar was answered by other roars of greeting.

There, standing before him, was Ballo the Great Lion. And gathered at his side were Tembo's mother, Marumbo, his father, Ganjo, his childhood friend, Junga, and many others who had gone before, including Omkhulu, who was greatly changed now that he was friends with Ballo. Tembo missed Jembo and his children a little bit, but he knew that at the right time they would join him there one day.

Tembo felt happy, for he was among those who loved him. He knew he had finished his quest on earth to bring peace to the Lion Kingdom. Now he was truly home, and here there was only love.

About the Author
& the Illustrator

Iain Gow left South Africa at age sixteen to go to school in Switzerland, then attended university in the United States for six years where he completed a Master's in Business Administration. Joining an international pharmaceutical/medical company, he spent time living in France, Brussels and the UK.

At 29, he felt the call of Christ to become an Anglican priest and, after training at Trinity College, Bristol, for four years, was ordained in Coventry Cathedral and worked as Assistant Rector at St Martin in the Bullring, Birmingham.

Since coming to New Zealand, he has worked as a chaplain at Kristin School (Auckland) and the Hibiscus Hospice (Orewa). Most recently, he has been the director of Vaughan Park Anglican Retreat Centre, Auckland (www. vaughanpark.org.nz). He has trained as a spiritual director with Spiritual Growth Ministries (NZ), and was co-founder of the Christian community, Without Walls.

Mark Rouse grew up as the son of a National Park Service Ranger in the USA. Every two or three years, his family moved from one beautiful national park to another, giving him a unique appreciation for wildlife and the natural world.

Having studied Fine Art at the University of Denver, he went on to CalArts, where he earned a degree in character animation. After a few years working on animated feature films, he shifted to the world of advertising (cargocollective.com/markrousecreative). Since then, he has created work for brands such as Honda, Ford and Weyerhaeuser, to name a few. He is now a creative director at Dailey (www.daileyla.com) in Los Angeles.

Mark (left) and Iain (right) in their young glory days.